HUGO SAVES CHRISTMAS ...IN MAY!

by Steven Hayet

HUGO SAVES CHRISTMAS…IN MAY!

SPECIAL NOTE

Anyone receiving permission to produce HUGO SAVES CHRISTMAS… IN MAY! is required to give credit to the Author as sole and exclusive Author of the Play on the title page of all programs distributed in connection with performances of the Play and in all instances in which the title of the Play appears for purposes of advertising, publicizing or otherwise exploiting the Play and/or a production thereof. The name of the Author must appear on a separate line, in which no other name appears, immediately beneath the title and in size of type equal to 50% of the size of the largest, most prominent letter used for the title of the Play. No person, firm, or entity may receive credit larger or more prominent than that accorded the Author.

SPECIAL NOTE ON SONGS AND RECORDINGS

For performances of copyrighted songs, arrangements or recordings mentioned in these Plays, the permission of the copyright owner(s) must be obtained. Other songs, arrangements or recordings may be substituted provided permission from the copyright owner(s) of such songs, arrangements or recordings is obtained; or songs, arrangements or recordings in the public domain may be substituted.

Book & Cover Design: Jonathan Cook
First Edition: March 2024
ISBN 978-1-7375216-5-5

"Christmas is the day that holds all time together."
- Alexander Smith, poet

"Christmas is a baby shower that went totally overboard."
- Andy Borowitz, writer

"Maybe Christmas, the Grinch thought, doesn't come from a store."
- Dr. Seuss, author

"A lovely thing about Christmas is that it's compulsory, like a thunderstorm, and we all go through it together."
- Garrison Keillor, author

HUGO SAVES CHRISTMAS…IN MAY! by Steven Hayet was commissioned by the Roaring Epiphany Production Company. The original workshop reading was held at the Alliance of Resident Theatres (A.R.T.), located at 520 8th Ave in NYC in August 2022. It was directed by Luci Samp and stage managed by Ashley Waldron. The cast was as follows:

HUGO MCGEE .... RJ VerChaud
MAYA KAPLAN .... Jillian Faye Liebman

HUGO SAVES CHRISTMAS…IN MAY! had its world premiere at Alchemical Studios, located at 50 W17th St. in NYC in May 2023. It was directed by REPC's Co-Artistic Directors, RJ VerChaud and Jillian Faye Liebman. The cast was as follows:

HUGO MCGEE .... Ethan Thomas
MAYA KAPLAN .... Lex E. Rojas
CATHERINE MCGEE .... Maxine Turenne
RACHEL KAPLAN .... Haley Rice

HUGO SAVES CHRISTMAS ...IN MAY!

CHARACTERS

HUGO MCGEE
Male, 30's. Gus from 'Psych' meets Dug from 'Up'.

MAYA KAPLAN
Female, 30's. Mila Kunis in 'A Bad Moms Christmas' meets Dante from 'Clerks'.

CATHERINE MCGEE
Hugo's mother.

RACHEL KAPLAN
Maya's mother, co-owner of Yuletide Cheer Holiday Store.

PLACE

Yuletide Cheer Holiday Store

TIME

Scene 1: Early May, present day

Scene 2: Two weeks later

Scene 3: Thirty years earlier

Scene 4: One year after Scene 1

NOTES

This play can be performed with or without an intermission. If the producing theatre prefers an intermission, after scene 2 is the most ideal spot.

The scene titles are just markers to separate the beats in the script.

SCENE 1

"I HATE CHRISTMAS"

It's a lovely spring day, but inside it's Christmas. The store is full of wreaths, plastic trees, ornaments and an assortment of Christmas gifts and accessories. It's a world of red and green. By the register sits a bellhop bell and a cordless phone.

Maya Kaplan packs decorations into a cardboard box. Filled to the brim, she picks it up and starts to carry it to the back room when the phone rings. She puts the box down, walks over and answers it.

MAYA. *(Into the phone with little enthusiasm.)* Yuletide Cheer Holiday Store. There's no place like here for the holidays. This is Maya. Ho-Ho-How can I help you? *(A few beats.)* Sorry, you have the wrong number. *(Beat.)* Yes, I'm sure. Did you want to call Yuletide Cheer? *(Beat.)* Then you have the wrong number - *(Beat.)* Humbug to you too sir. *(To herself.)* I hate Christmas. *(She picks up the box and exits. Hugo McGee enters the front door. This is his happy place. He browses his way over to a tree full of ornaments. After a quick perusal, he spots the one he was looking for. He walks over to the register. No one is there. He looks around and his eyes rest on the bellhop bell. He rings it. No one appears. He rings it again. Inspiration strikes. He begins to sing while accompanying himself on the bellhop bell.)*

HUGO. *(Singing to himself.)*
HARK HOW THE BELLS
SWEET SILVER BELLS
ALL SEEM TO SAY
THROW CARES AWAY
(Maya enters carrying an empty cardboard box and a clipboard. Hugo doesn't notice. He continues singing.)
CHRISTMAS IS HERE
BRINGING GOOD CHEER
TO YOUNG AND OLD
MEEK AND THE BOLD

MAYA. *(Setting the box down.)* Can I help you?

HUGO. Oh, I'm sorry. I just got carried away. Merry Christmas!

MAYA. *(Matter-of-factly.)* It's May.

HUGO. Not in here. Here it's always Christmas.

MAYA. That it is.

HUGO. Do you know where the dollar ornaments are?

MAYA. *(Pointing to a decorated box.)* Over there.

HUGO. Ahh. I see it. Thank you! *(Admiring the store décor as he makes his way to the box.)* This place looks almost exactly as I remember it. Though I remember the tree being bigger, probably because I was smaller. Oh, and I remember a mailbox sitting over here. It had candy cane stripes. I'd drop off my letter to the North Pole.

MAYA. We put that away a few years ago. Kids just stopped using it. They can email Santa now. I even heard there was a number where you can text him.

HUGO. Are you serious?

MAYA. Yeah. I'm sure it's just a bot with standard phrases, but if I were a kid, I'd definitely try to mess with it. I'd ask for crazy things likes world peace or a box of throwing stars, just to see what the response would be.

HUGO. Blocked, reported, and a lump of coal. *(Arriving at*

the box, Hugo sits on the floor. As he talks, he takes out the ornaments, examines them, and plays with them like when he was a child. His eye catches a particular ornament.) Oooh, that's cute. My mom used to take me here when I was little every year. She'd do most of the shopping but I was allowed to pick one new ornament for the tree from the dollar ornament section. She told me that it was the most important job.

Catherine appears in a vignette.

CATHERINE. Hugo, I need you to focus. This is big. You know how Christmas is the most special time of year? We need to make it special for Santa too. Santa always visits the same houses year after year and we don't want him to get bored seeing the same old ornaments. I need you to search this box and pick the most interesting ornament. And what's that? How will you know which one is the most interesting? Pick something that catches your eye. Maybe it's shiny. Maybe it's got fun colors. If you like it and find it interesting, Santa will love it … and his Christmas will be wonderful.

End vignette.

HUGO. *(To Maya.)* So my whole childhood, I believed that I kept Santa interested in his job. Pretty funny story, right?

MAYA. Oh. I wasn't listening.

HUGO. I can repeat it.

MAYA. That's okay.

HUGO. What was the last thing you remember hearing?

MAYA. "Do you know where the dollar ornaments are?"

HUGO. You weren't paying attention?

MAYA. I was busy.

HUGO. It was a really good story.

MAYA. I'm sorry, sir, but -

HUGO. Hugo. Sir was my father's name.

MAYA. Okay Hugo -wait- Your father's name was "sir?"

HUGO. Yeah that didn't work. If you had said Mr. McGee, then that would have landed better. I was thinking of the punchline before the setup. That's like putting a star on the tree before any ornaments.

MAYA. Good thing you're buying ornaments.

HUGO. Yeah, my mom used to take me here as a kid.

MAYA. You already mentioned that.

HUGO. So you were listening!

MAYA. I caught a little.

HUGO. Then why did you lie. Lying will get you a lump of coal from Santa Claus.

MAYA. Lucky for me then that Santa's not real.

HUGO. *(Over the top shocked.)* How could you say that!?! Such lies! Such slander! You dare defame jolly old St. Nick? *(Whispers.)* There are no kids in here, right?

MAYA. You see anyone else in the store?

HUGO. I just wanted to be safe. Kids are sneaky. They can hide anywhere. And the last thing I'd want to do is destroy a child's Christmas spirit.

MAYA. Don't worry. You're good.

HUGO. It happened once. I was in 3rd grade. I had already figured out the secret - my mom slipped up one year and left the very same wrapping paper out in the hall closet that Santa used. Now every kid knows that Santa doesn't have the time to wrap the gifts that night - between the gift delivery and the massive amount of cookies he has to consume. That's when I deduced that it had to be my mom. But I kept it secret. Because Christmas spirit.

MAYA. Obviously. Christmas spirit.

HUGO. Until one day at lunch - it was our first day back from winter vacation - Danny Sariotis was making fun of other poorer kids' gifts and bragging about the Xbox Santa had brought him and I had had enough of his bullying. I said "Danny, Santa's not real." He looked confused. I then realized you can't just drop that information bomb without an explanation. So I looked him right in the eye and told him he was such a mean kid, making fun of other kids' presents, that if Santa was real, there's not a chance he'd get an Xbox. His parents bought it for him so Danny could spend hours in his room and they wouldn't have to deal with the monster he'd become.

MAYA. Did he cry?

HUGO. No. He punched me right in the face ... which just served as further confirmation that Santa wasn't real. In a just world, monsters would not get Xbox's.

MAYA. I agree with you there.

HUGO. When did you learn that Santa wasn't real?

MAYA. Me?

HUGO. Yeah. How old were you? When did you know?

MAYA. Ehh. I guess always? I never believed in Santa.

HUGO. Never? That's crazy.

MAYA. Did you decide what you are getting?

HUGO. No, I'm still trying to get over the whole never-believing-in-Santa? How did you grow up with any sense of wonder and joy?

MAYA. I managed somehow.

HUGO. A Christmas miracle!

MAYA. A Christmas miracle.

HUGO. Because I can't imagine someone wanting to work here and not feeling constantly overwhelmed with joy -

MAYA. I'm sorry, sir - Hugo -

HUGO. You called me Sir Hugo, like I'm a knight! *(Swinging an imaginary sword.)* Yaaaah!

MAYA. *(Interrupting.)* Hugo. Can you decide what you want to buy ... to yourself? I'm happy to help you if you have questions, but I have a lot of work to do.

HUGO. Wow. Work work work. I guess you didn't get any wonder and joy after-all.

MAYA. Excuse me?

HUGO. That was rude of me. I'll buy something soon. I'm just torn between these two.

MAYA. Why not get both? Everything's half off.

HUGO. Half off? The one-dollar ornaments are always one dollar. That's what makes them the dollar ornaments.

MAYA. It's clearance pricing. We're closing up shop in a couple weeks.

HUGO. For the summer?

MAYA. For good.

HUGO. That's not possible. This store has been around for...for like 40 years.

MAYA. We had a good run.

HUGO. Yuletide Cheer cannot close, especially in the middle of May.

MAYA. Would you prefer the middle of June?

HUGO. You don't seem remotely upset about this.

MAYA. Not particularly.

HUGO. I want to speak to someone who cares. There has to be someone who cares. Can you get the manager?

MAYA. Are you seriously pulling that card?

HUGO. Yes. I'd like to talk to the manager.

MAYA. I am the manager.

HUGO. Then the owner. You know what I mean. I want to talk to the owner, the sweet older lady with the holly brooch. I want to talk to her.

MAYA. She's not in.

HUGO. And when will she be in next?

MAYA. Never.

HUGO. *(Thinking she's passed.)* Oh my God. Oh my God. I'm so sorry. I didn't make -

MAYA. *(Realizing.)* Oh, no. No no no. She's fine … ish. She's in Florida with my brother.

HUGO. So you're her -

MAYA. Daughter, yeah. I'm Maya. We've been trying to get Mom to retire for a while now, but she's crazy stubborn. Then a couple months ago, she tripped on a toy train. Now she's in Florida recovering and I'm here running the store full time.

HUGO. I'm so sorry.

MAYA. Thanks. It's not the worst job I could have.

HUGO. I meant for your mom.

MAYA. Why? She's in Florida probably lounging by my brother's pool.

HUGO. But she's your mother!

MAYA. She's fine. She's alive. What's there to be sorry about? Fun fact: If she had died, we wouldn't have to worry about the rest of the lease. Isn't that sad? It's so much cheaper in this country to be dead. I get what George Bailey was thinking.

HUGO. That is an absolutely awful thing to say.

MAYA. I don't wish she was dead. I just recognize the irony.

HUGO. In a way, it worked out better for you. You got to spend more time working at the best job on Earth.

MAYA. I wouldn't say that.

HUGO. Okay, I'll rephrase. Best real job on Earth. There are lots of fictional jobs that would be way cooler. When I was little, my mom gave me the job as the Cookie Sheriff.

> *Catherine appears in a vignette, holding a tray of cookies.*

CATHERINE. Don't these smell delicious? Fresh out of the oven. This is always the hard part. These cookies are for Santa and we need to make sure they don't get eaten before he gets here. *(She pulls a dollar store cowboy badge out of her pocket.)* I need your help. You are being deputized. The official Cookie Sheriff of Christmas. There are twenty-three cookies here. You keep them safe from anyone who tries to take one - bandits, outlaws, hungry mommies - then as your reward, Sheriff Hugo, I'll make sure you get all the extra cookies that Santa didn't eat. How does that sound, partner?

> *End vignette.*

HUGO. My mom would always make Snickerdoodles, which also happened to be my favorite. What's your favorite kind of cookie? I can always tell a lot about a person by the kind of cookie they like.

MAYA. Hugo, I have a ton of work to do. I'll be in the back. *(Hugo looks around the store nostalgically. Maya gathers some things and starts to exit.)*

HUGO. It's really a shame. Another local institution disappearing.

MAYA. Yup. But we'll all be okay. Ring if you need me. *(As soon as she's about to exit, Hugo has an idea and rings the bell. Maya is exasperated.)* Yes?

HUGO. Have you ever gone through life wondering what your purpose is only to have it suddenly become crystal clear why you were put on this Earth?

MAYA. No. *(Off his look.)* I'm assuming you just have.

HUGO. Yes! Thank you for asking. I am going to save this store. That's why I'm here. Only need to figure out the how, but I will do it.

MAYA. Please don't.

HUGO. I will.

MAYA. I appreciate you caring, but don't.

HUGO. This store is an institution. I would not be the

person I am today without it! This town needs a place where Christmas can be celebrated every single day.

MAYA. Have you ever seen the movie *Groundhog Day*?

HUGO. Yeah.

MAYA. Replace it with Christmas and that's my life.

HUGO. A classic that stands the test of time?

MAYA. Christmas is supposed to be special. A once-a-year thing to look forward to. When day after day after day after day I'm force-fed jolly and subjected to the same Christmas carols over and over and over - I swear- it loses the magic. The human mind is not evolved to withstand hearing "Dominick the Donkey" once let alone multiple times a day, every single day. It's how serial killers are created.

HUGO. Maya … that's not how serial killers are created. Serial killers come from lack of purpose … and from getting forgotten in too many games of hide and seek. But don't worry. You can trust me. I have my purpose. I'm going to save Christmas. *(Building with excitement like a snowball turning into an avalanche of enthusiasm.)* "Now, Dasher! Now, Dancer! Now, Prancer and Vixen! On, Comet! On Cupid! On, Donder and Blitzen! To the top of the porch! To the top of the wall! Now dash away! Dash away! Dash away all!" *(He exits.)*

MAYA. I really hate Christmas. *("Dominick the Donkey" begins to play on the store radio.)* Humbug.

    End of scene.

SCENE 2

"THANK YOU FOR THE GOOD MEMORIES"

Two weeks later. Hugo, wearing a backpack, darts into the store and beelines straight to the register. He rings the bellhop bell repeatedly like a child trying to get his mother's attention. Maya quickly leaps out brandishing a giant candy cane for protection.

MAYA. *(Recognizing him.)* What the Hell, Harry!

HUGO. It's Hugo -

MAYA. I don't care! I thought I was about to get robbed. You can't just burst into a store like that.

HUGO. *(He has exciting news.)* I did it.

MAYA. You are lucky I didn't belt you. This thing is plastic, but it's a hard plastic. It'd give you a hell of a bruise.

HUGO. Maya, I did it.

MAYA. Did what? Nearly give me a heart attack? Yeah, you did.

HUGO. No. I raised the money.

MAYA. What money?

HUGO. To save the store!

MAYA. No. No no. I didn't ask you to do that.

HUGO. I wanted to. You're George Bailey. I'm Mary and I rallied the town! *(Singing.)*
  SHOULD AULD ACQUAINTANCE BE FORGOT
   AND NEVER BROUGHT TO MIND.

MAYA. *(Overlapping with Hugo's singing.)* Hugo, no.

Wait. Can you just -

HUGO. Sing with me, Maya. *(Singing again.)*
        SHOULD AULD ACQUAINTANCE BE FORGOT
… *(Disappointed.)* Why aren't you singing? *(Has a realization.)* Oh yeah. He walks over to the bell and rings it. Hear that? An angel got its wings!

MAYA. Hugo, can you stop singing - please - and explain to me what you've done?

HUGO. I went around town and rallied the community! The store is saved! The community wasn't going to let Yuletide Cheer disappear. *(Chuckles to himself.)* That rhymed.

MAYA. What do you mean "rallied the community?" They aren't outside are they? Are they?! Dammit. *(She runs quickly off stage and after a beat she returns relieved.)* There's no one there. Thank God. This is the second heart attack you've given me in the last five minutes.

HUGO. This has been an exciting day. You woke up today thinking this local institution was coming to a close, but now you know it's not!

MAYA. Hugo, the store is going to close.

HUGO. It can't, Maya.

MAYA. It will. Nothing will change that. I'm really sorry to disappoint you and the community.

HUGO. Can I be honest with you?

MAYA. *(Wryly.)* Like you haven't been?

HUGO. I went around the entire town. I knocked on doors, I called local businesses, I even set up a table outside the supermarket to catch shoppers as they left. Boy, those girl-scouts were PISSED that I took their spot. The community didn't want to help. There was one old man who lectured me about bailouts and not interfering with capitalism, like it was the time-space continuum. Here's the thing - I don't care. I'm not going to be deterred. I'd rather have an army but if I have fight this war to save Christmas solo, then call me Yuletide Rambo. *(Considers.)* Actually, that's a dumb name. Please don't call me that. *(He opens his backpack, pulls out a loose wad of cash and places it on the table. There are crumbled bills and maybe a few coins.)* This should be about five hundred dollars. It's all I have liquid right at the moment. However, here is the pièce de résistance. *(He reaches into his backpack and pulls out an action figure. He has a quick second thought about putting it back in his backpack, but there is no turning back. He presents it to Maya.)* It's a limited-edition Star Wars Admiral Akbar action figure, still in its original packaging. In this condition, if you were to sell it in twenty or thirty years, this will be worth tens of thousands of dollars easy. This should cover another six months of rent and by that time, it'll be Christmas, and it'll be your busy season, and we'll sell so much stuff that -

MAYA. Hugo, this is incredibly sweet. Really, it is. But I can't accept these.

HUGO. It's a gift. To this store. To your mom. From me and my family to yours.

MAYA. This isn't right.

HUGO. I know. I know. You feel awkward because I gave you the best Christmas gift ever but know I want to.

MAYA. It's not that.

HUGO. It's not the best Christmas gift ever? *(A realization.)* Did you get a pony? You got a pony, didn't you? I didn't think people actually got ponies –

MAYA. No.

HUGO. It was a Power Wheels! That makes way more sense than a pony. I always wanted one, but my mom would say that if I wanted to drive a car 5mph, I can move to New York when I grew up, and sit in the Holland Tunnel traffic during rush hour.

MAYA. Will you let me actually talk?! Good God! Your

mind is answering questions that no one is asking. I'm flattered by how much you care about this store. My mom would be touched to know that her little shop had this impact on you. Truly. But there is nothing that can be done. Yuletide Cheer will be closing its doors. I'm sorry. I'm sorry you went to all this effort. I'm sorry you annoyed girl scouts and got yelled at by a bitter old man. I'm just sorry, but what's done is done. *(Hugo is taken aback, like a boxer who catches a right, but he regroups.)*

HUGO. I knew this was a possibility. I had a sense. When I left the store two weeks ago, a part of me knew that even if I pulled off the Christmas miracle of raising the funds to keep this store afloat, you still may need convincing.

MAYA. There is nothing to convince me of.

HUGO. You may need ... a second Christmas miracle. Fortunately for me, I always come prepared. Maya, I know why this store is closing.

MAYA. Yes, because I literally told you. My mom. Slipped on a toy train. Now in Florida.

HUGO. No. It's because you lost your Christmas spirit! Don't worry. I'll help you find it using a time-tested method. Consider me the Ghost of Christmas Past!

MAYA. What?

HUGO. The Ghost of Christmas Past ... from *A Christmas Carol*?

MAYA. I know the story. I'm confused by your plan. You can time travel?

HUGO. No, but I have an internet connection. I Googled your name. Now, we can see the full picture of what makes you, Maya, the metaphorical lump of coal in our community's Christmas stocking.

MAYA. This is really creepy.

HUGO. They are public records. It's not like I know where you live. *(Reading.)* "Maya. Kaplan, age 34, lives at 14

Branford Street" - Okay, I know where you live, but it's not like I would ever go there. I just want to lead you on a Scrooge-like transformation and save Christmas ... that is all.

MAYA. Fine. I'll play along if it gets you to leave sooner. What else does it say there? Anything about where I hid the bodies?

HUGO. Very funny. It says you have no criminal record.

MAYA. No known criminal record. Because I'm good at my job.

HUGO. Can you please humor me? I'm trying to help you find the Christmas spirit! By examining your past, we'll learn about the events that led you down this path of humbuggery.

MAYA. Humbuggery?

HUGO. *(Reading.)* "Maya Kaplan, Age 34, lives at 14 Branford Street. No criminal record. Occupation: Unknown."

MAYA. *(Gestures around.)* You serious?

HUGO. *(Reading.)* "Parents: Mark and Rachel. Sibling: Seth."

MAYA. This is really digging deep. It's like you've know me my whole life.

HUGO. There is more! *(Scanning the paper.)* Wait. Boring. Boring. What? I don't think this is accurate - It says your net worth is 14 million dollars.

MAYA. *(Sarcastically.)* That's totally accurate. I'm loaded. I just work here for fun!

HUGO. It also says you're Jewish.

MAYA. That part's right at least.

HUGO. You're Jewish?

MAYA. I know.

HUGO. Are you joking?

MAYA. Why would I joke about that?

HUGO. So you're a Jewish millionaire?

MAYA. Not a millionaire. That is a stereotype.

HUGO. But your mother owned the store. Your mother -

MAYA. Is also Jewish. That's typically how it works in Judaism.

HUGO. But she owned a Christmas Store.

MAYA. Should she have owned a deli?

HUGO. No - I mean - you don't see how it's weird?

MAYA. Weird?

HUGO. Not common.

MAYA. Growing up, this was the only Christmas store I heard of, so I believed they were all run by Jews. I mean, many Christmas songs were written by Jews so it wasn't that big of a stretch.

HUGO. No they weren't.

MAYA. Absolutely they were. All the best ones.

HUGO. A Jew wrote "The Christmas Shoes"?

MAYA. No. Do you really think that's the best Christmas song?

HUGO. *(Embarrassed.)* I don't now.

MAYA. "Rudolph the Red Nosed Reindeer". "Silver Bells". Literally "The Christmas Song" – Chestnuts roasting blah blah blah - THE Christmas Song. I practically hear more Jewish music working here than I do when I'm in shul.

HUGO. I'm still processing the first thing. Why did your mom decide to own a Christmas store?

MAYA. Why not?

HUGO. Why not is not a reason. It's the answer you give when you don't want to give one. Why did you eat an entire meat lover's pizza? Why not? Why did you get a pet scorpion? Why not? Why did you play in traffic? Why not? "Why not" is only slightly better than "because I said so."

MAYA. I don't have to give you a reason.

HUGO. I'm not forcing you, but I'm genuinely interested.

MAYA. My mom and her friend wanted to run a business. The store was for sale. They took chance. After a couple years, the friend left. Mom didn't. Fast forward two decades and here we are. It's not exciting. No one is bidding for the movie rights.

HUGO. Was your mom's friend ... also?

MAYA. You can say Jewish. And no, she wasn't. She was just an old friend. Not sure how they met. It was before I was born. Best friends but horrible business partners. They had creative differences. Patty - the friend - always wanted to go crazy over the top with decorations and inflatable Santas and all that stuff. My mom wanted a classier approach. Classic. White lights. Candles - electric, not real ones. We're not about to cause a fire.

HUGO. Makes sense.

Rachel appears in a vignette.

RACHEL. Maya, did you sort that box of candy cane ornaments?

MAYA. I'm working on it.

RACHEL. Can you pick up the pace? We're going to be late to pick Seth up at soccer practice.

MAYA. It's hard. There's this giant old-lady mannequin blocking the shelves.

RACHEL. That wasn't my idea. Patty wanted to do a window display dedicated to that Grandma Got Run Over by a Reindeer song.

MAYA. Did you tell Patty it's a dumb idea?

RACHEL. I did.

MAYA. Are you okay mom?

RACHEL. I'm fine, Maya.

MAYA. Mom, you can tell me. I'm thirteen. I'm an adult now.

RACHEL. When I say I'm fine that means I'm fine. Some people just don't have the Christmas spirit. Now let's get going. We don't want your brother to be left behind.

End of vignette.

MAYA. Apparently, their argument got heated and personal and ended with Patty screaming on her way out the door, "What does a Jew know about Christmas?"

HUGO. Geesh.

MAYA. Yep. And Mom's been running the store solo since. And "what does a Jew know about Christmas?" Christmas is literally a Jew's birthday party and Patty was at my Bat Mitzvah. She knows firsthand my mom can throw a Hell of a party.

HUGO. I went to a Bar Mitzvah once for my friend. We did the circle dance and then he got lifted up in the chair. That looked absolutely terrifying. Is it always the four drunkest cousins who volunteer to hold the chair?

MAYA. Sometimes you get the uncle with the bad knee, but no one who should be lifting you in a chair is ever the one lifting the chair. I think it's why they say that's when you become an adult. Sitting in that chair, being raised up and down while being spun in circles ... that was the first time I truly had to deal with my own mortality.

HUGO. So this store - it obviously means a lot to your mom.

MAYA. It always came first. When my friends got to hang out on weekends, I had to work here. While my brother got to go to sleep away camp, I had to work here. When my mom slipped and fell on that train and hurt her leg, her first call was to me -

HUGO. That's a start.

MAYA. - to ask me to cover the store so she could go to the

hospital. And by "cover" she meant "a year of my life."

HUGO. And why hasn't your brother ever helped you with any of this?

MAYA. Because I'm single and childless.

HUGO. I don't get why that matters.

MAYA. Hugo, are you married?

HUGO. No.

MAYA. Then get married. Get married yesterday. And have children. It doesn't matter the number, just pop out a kid. Because if your siblings get married before you, then your life and your dreams become forfeit and you are conscripted into a life of geriatric care. Your parents will never bother your siblings because they have families but your time doesn't matter. And if you dare appear hesitant in any way, you will get a sermon on selfishness and parental sacrifices. Don't get me wrong, I'm grateful my parents paid my college tuition, but if I knew that they'd prevent me from taking any opportunity where I can use the degree, I would have saved them the money and had a clear conscience.

HUGO. So your dream was not to work in holiday retail?

MAYA. I wanted to be a zoologist. Study animals in the wild. Take care of them in sanctuaries. But that dream effectively ended on September 4, 2006.

HUGO. What happened?

MAYA. Steve Irwin was killed by a stingray. My mom was already uneasy when Roy got mauled by his tiger but this put her over the edge.

Rachel appears in a vignette.

RACHEL. No, Maya. Absolutely not.

MAYA. Mom!

RACHEL. This is insanity. A man died!

MAYA. He's like the second person in Australia to ever be

killed by a stingray.

RACHEL. And why do you want to be number three so badly?

MAYA. I don't even like stingrays.

RACHEL. That's not the point, Maya, and you know it. Today it's a stingray. Tomorrow it'll be a bear or a shark or an elephant. And while you're off roaming the world trying to befriend these beasts that only see you as a talking porterhouse, I'm not getting any younger. What if something were to happen? And don't say you know nothing will happen because you don't know. Everyone thinks they are so smart and knows everything, but if they did, why would there be Emergency Rooms then? Think about that one, Miss "I'm Not Going to Get Attacked by a Stingray."

End vignette.

MAYA. Anytime I'd bring up to my mom about taking a job somewhere that'd involve animals, she'd give me a whole spiel about the store and all the things that could potentially happen to her if I'm gone. And I knew she'd be fine. Statistically. Logically. I knew. But I couldn't risk it. The guilt. It's been programmed into me. Years and years of conditioning. It's crazy. Everyone will die. We know that. But if she happened to die while I'm taking care of animals in New Zealand or wherever, I would spend the rest of my life believing I could have saved her from that tornado. Yes, one of the examples she gave me is that she - and the store - would get caught in a tornado. But I know - with absolute confidence - that if she were on her death bed and I was sitting right next to her, holding in her hand, looking her right in the eyes, her last words would be, "Where's your brother?" All Seth has to do is send a photo of his children and a sample of their chicken scratch crayon artwork and say "they made it for their grandma!" and he's now child of the year. But for me, I have to choose. The dilemma of the unmarried childless child: Either serve your parents until they die and sacrifice all your dreams OR know that the day they do die, it'll be your fault somehow and that you could have done more. So here I am. Choosing door number one. My dreams. At least for a few more weeks.

HUGO. There is a door number three.

MAYA. Enlighten me.

HUGO. You can change your dreams.

MAYA. Brilliant.

HUGO. You are looking at life like you are at a crossroad when there are really many paths you can explore. Life is rarely a binary either/or. You can have your cake and eat it too. Maybe it just involves eating a little less cake.

MAYA. And I assume my new dream involves me somehow working at the store?

HUGO. I am merely the Ghost of Christmas past. I do not tell you your dreams. I just provide guidance.

MAYA. You're as useful as a magic eight ball.

HUGO. What's your favorite animal?

MAYA. What's that got to do with anything?

HUGO. What's your favorite animal?

MAYA. The beluga whale.

HUGO. Really? Darn. I hoped you would say a camel. A goat or a donkey would have also worked.

MAYA. We are not getting a live nativity scene.

HUGO. It's a valid option. A win-win for both of us! I get Christmas. You get your animal fix.

MAYA. No. You get Christmas. I have to deal with the liability of some kid getting kicked by a camel when trying to take a selfie.

HUGO. It would be fun! And people add all kinds of fun animals to their mangers, like parrots and monkeys. I'm sure we could figure out a way to add a beluga whale.

MAYA. If I'm going to turn this store into an aquarium, why don't I just work at the aquarium?

HUGO. Think about it. The path is clear as day: Beluga. Baby Beluga. Baby. Baby in a manger. Away in a Manger. Christmas Carol. Christmas Store. There you go!

MAYA. *(Completely over it.)* I want to live my own dreams, Hugo. Not your dreams. Not my mother's dreams. Not some altered scaled-down off-brand dollar-store knock off of my dreams. My dreams. What I set out to do. I'm going to be selfish for once. For the first time in years, I have the opportunity to be happy and I want to be happy!

HUGO. Okay. I think that's a good place to end this journey to the past. It was nostalgic. It was introspective. It was informative and lets us know who you were, so we can discover who you will be. Let's put a big check next to Ghost of Christmas Past. Now to the Ghost of Christmas Present: We're here right now, in the present, so look around, pretty store, oooh - see the ornaments - look that's a tree! - and check! That was an easy one. And now for the finale: The Ghost of Christmas Yet to Come.

MAYA. Are you almost done?

HUGO. Last one! *(Opening his bag and pulling out a robe.)* I don't own a creepy cloak. The closest I have are these Hogwarts robes I got for LeakyCon last year, but just imagine I'm the Ghost of Christmas Yet to Come and not Percy Weasley.

MAYA. That won't be too hard.

HUGO. Okay, here I go. *(Hugo puts on the robe, slowly turns to Maya, and points, with a silent deliberate intensity. Maya is not sure what he is pointing at, but he does not flinch. She looks at Hugo, then to where he's pointing, then back to Hugo.)*

MAYA. *(In a Maggie Smith-esque accent.)* What is a

student doing roaming the halls at these hours? A prefect no less! 10 points from Gryffindor and don't let it happen again!

HUGO. Ugh. You are not taking this seriously!

MAYA. What do you expect me to do? You're just standing there and pointing!

HUGO. That's what this ghost does! He stands, and he points, and he's ominous. That's his thing. But at the end of the day, it works because Scrooge sees the error of his ways and buys a sick kid a turkey. *(Pointing.)* Do you see the error of your ways?

MAYA. I'm not buying you a turkey.

HUGO. *(Pointing intensely.)* Do you see the error of your ways?

MAYA. *(Insincerely.)* I do. But there is no undoing the past. According to the great philosopher Cher, it is impossible to turn back time.

HUGO. *(Pointing even more intensely.)* Look harder. Do you see the error of your ways?

MAYA. No.

HUGO. Then what do you see?!?

MAYA. *(Faux gazing.)* I see ... I see … a Starbucks!

HUGO. A what?

MAYA. A Starbucks. In a few months' time, this storefront will be the proud location of the fourth Starbucks in a two-mile radius.

HUGO. You are joking.

MAYA. Paperwork has already been filed with the city.

HUGO. *(Stunned disbelief.)* No no no no no no no no no no no no. A Starbucks?! You are replacing this Christmas store with a Starbucks?

MAYA. I'm not personally. They chose to move in here. Secretly, I was rooting for a Chipotle.

HUGO. But we got a Starbucks! The most anti-Christmas store there is! How can you walk into a Starbucks and know it's Christmas time? Besides the cups being red, and the assortment of peppermint flavored beverages, and the non-stop playing of Michael Bublé Christmas albums. We're going from an always Christmas store to a sometimes Christmas store.

MAYA. Christmas is a sometimes holiday. My mom owns a 365-day store that celebrates a one-day event. If you go by the song, twelve days tops.

HUGO. It's more than twelve days. It's a season. From Thanksgiving to New Years. No. Even longer. I could swear that I started hearing Christmas songs on the radio before Halloween. But it's more than that. Christmas is a mindset. It's a feeling of happiness and cheer. There's a song from *Hello Dolly* -

MAYA. It's *Mame*.

HUGO. You sure?

MAYA. I hear the song 14 times a day. I'm sure. "We Need a Little Christmas" is from *Mame*.

HUGO. Then you get the idea. When we need happiness and a pick-me-up, Christmas is that pick-me-up, and I don't know about you, but a place where I can find happiness and cheer shouldn't be a sometimes store.

MAYA. Then how come I've never seen you here before.

HUGO. I was here two weeks ago.

MAYA. You know what I meant. Before then! Why have I never seen you?

HUGO. I didn't have a specific need for happiness and cheer then, but it's good to know that your store is there in case I do.

MAYA. I'm sorry, Hugo, but I am not going to give up my life just on the off chance that you need some holiday cheer on a random Tuesday in the middle of May. It's absurd for you to ask.

HUGO. I'm sorry it has come to this, Maya. *(Hugo reaches into his backpack, pulls out a set of handcuffs and cuffs himself to the Christmas tree.)*

MAYA. What are you doing?

HUGO. I am not going anywhere until I know that Yuletide Cheer is not going anywhere.

MAYA. Which Christmas story is this from? I don't remember one with a crazy person tying themself to a tree!

HUGO. Commence: Operation Christmas Spirit!

MAYA. Good grief.

HUGO. *(Singing loudly.)*

> *GOOD KING WENCESLAS LOOKED OUT*
> *TO THE VIRGIN MOTHER*
> *WHEN THE SNOW LAY ROUND ABOUT*
> *DEEP AND CRISPIN GLOVER*

MAYA. Crispin Glover? That's not even the right lyrics.

HUGO. I'm pretty sure it is.
(Singing.)

> *DEEP AND CRISPIN GLOVER*

MAYA. Crispin Glover is the dad from *Back to the Future*. It goes -
(Singing.)

> *GOOD KING WENCESLAS LOOKED OUT*
> *TO THE VIRGIN MOTHER*
> *WHEN THE SNOW LAY ROUND ABOUT*
> *DEEP AND CRISP AND EVEN*

HUGO. Oh you want to sing! Are you getting the Christmas Spirit?
(Singing.)

> *BRIGHTLY SHONE THE MOON THAT NIGHT*
> *THOUGH THE FROST WAS CRUEL*

MAYA. *(Interrupting.)* Nice try! We're not doing this. I

have work to do, and I am going to do it, so that I don't have to stay in this store any longer than I have to.

HUGO. Then I will just entertain myself through the power of song.

(Singing.)

> *ON THE FIRST DAY OF CHRISTMAS*
> *MY TRUE LOVE SENT TO ME*
> *A PARTRIDGE IN A PEAR TREE!*
> *ON THE SECOND DAY OF CHRISTMAS*

MAYA. Very clever. Do you think you can break me with that? You forget. I am Jewish. Ever been to a Passover seder? We invented songs with too many verses!

HUGO. This isn't the "Twelve Days of Christmas". That wouldn't make sense. We're in Yuletide Cheer, where Christmas is every day! This is the "Three Hundred and Sixty-Five Days of Christmas"! I'll skip to my favorite verse.

(Singing.)

> *ON THE ONE HUNDRED FORTY-NINTH DAY OF*
> *CHRISTMAS*
> *MY TRUE LOVE GAVE TO ME*
> *ONE HUNDRED FORTY-NINE BARS OF CHOCOLATE*
> *ONE HUNDRED FORTY-EIGHT CUPS OF OATMEAL*
> *ONE HUNDRED FORTY-SEVEN BEANIE BABIES*
> *ONE HUNDRED FORTY-SIX LAMBORGHINIS*
> *ONE HUNDRED FORTY-FIVE OLIVE GARDEN*
> *BREADSTICKS*
> *(Deep breath.)*
> *ONE HUNDRED FORTY-FOR HAIRLESS KITTENS*
> *ONE HUDRED -*

MAYA. Wait! I have it!

HUGO. What?

MAYA. I have it. I have the Christmas spirit! I am overjoyed. I want to sip cocoa and sing carols and demand figgy pudding from strangers and do all the best Christmas traditions.

HUGO. That's wonderful!

MAYA. And I want to start with my favorite Christmas tradition: opening presents. *(She picks up the Star Wars figure.)* I can't wait to open this one.

HUGO. You wouldn't.

MAYA. Watch me.

HUGO. But if you do that, it'll lose all its value. A toy is not meant to be touched by human hands!

MAYA. It's Christmas, Hugo. Are you going to deprive me the joy of opening presents?

HUGO. Don't. Please.

MAYA. Uncuff yourself from my Christmas tree and leave this store, or the toy gets it.

HUGO. You are a Grinch. *(He thinks about uncuffing himself, then decides against it. He grabs the tree and drags it with him as he chases after Maya.)* Give me my limited-edition collectible!

MAYA. Not a chance. *(Hugo pursues, but she easily stays ahead of him because he's lugging a tree.)*

HUGO. All I want to do is help!

MAYA. I never asked for your help. I don't need your help. I don't want your help. *(They circle the store, weaving in and out of different obstacles.)*

HUGO. Yes you do! You need me to save Christmas!

MAYA. You are being held back by Christmas.

HUGO. No I'm not.

MAYA. That wasn't a metaphor. Look at yourself. You are literally so tied to Christmas that you are unable to move forward. You want your life back, Hugo? *(She holds out the figure, mocking him.)* You're going to have to free yourself to get it. *(Hugo lunges for it, falling short, and tumbling over the tree. Maya races to the counter, pulls out scissors, and holds it up to the action figure like she's taken a hostage.)*

HUGO. *(Winded.)* Please. Don't open it. *(He uncuffs himself from the tree, stands up, and puts his hands in the air.)*

MAYA. Now get out of my store. *(Defeated, Hugo picks up the tree and stands it upright. He puts a few ornaments that fell on the ground during the kerfuffle back on the tree.)* Your mom would be embarrassed if she saw you like this.

HUGO. My mom passed away in February.

MAYA. What?

HUGO. She died last February.

MAYA. I'm so sorry.

HUGO. It's okay. You didn't know.

MAYA. But I didn't mean to be jerk.

HUGO. You did, but you didn't know, so you didn't mean to be that kind of jerk. That's why I said it was okay.

MAYA. I'm really sorry about your mother.

HUGO. Her birthday was two-weeks ago - would have been two-weeks ago - whatever- it was a rough day. They are all rough. Not a single day goes by when I don't think about her.

MAYA. It'll take time.

HUGO. I know. I'm told it gets easier but it hasn't yet, and to be honest, I'm wasn't sure if I want it to. I was worried that if it stopped hurting, that meant she no longer mattered as much. That day I passed this store. And I remembered the times Mom would bring me here when I was little - how I would always get to pick out a new ornament for the tree - and it made me smile. It was the first time I thought about her and I wasn't sad. Christmas was always just me and mom. My dad died when I was really really little. I don't really remember much about him, just that I've been told I sound like him when I laugh and that we both have terrible poker faces. I have two half-sisters - they were from his first marriage and are much older than me - so every Christmas, they'd spend it with their mom and I'd spend it with mine. This store is more than just four walls full of ornaments, candy canes, and other trinkets. It's full of memories. Some of my favorite. I lost my mom. I didn't want to lose the memories that went with her. I don't want to forget her. I don't want her to be forgotten. I'm sorry for taking your time. I'll go now. *(He puts his things in his backpack and starts to walk to the exit. Suddenly, he turns back to Maya.)* Maya?

MAYA. Yeah?

HUGO. Can I have my limited-edition Admiral Akbar action figure back? I know I gave it to you but -

MAYA. Sure. Of course. *(She walks over, hands him the figure and then remembers.)* Oh, your money. *(Walking back to the counter.)* Let me get that.

HUGO. No, that's okay. Give it to your mom as a thank you.

MAYA. It's five hundred dollars.

HUGO. She can buy herself a nice Christmas present. Tell her Catherine McGee's kid says, "Thank you for the good memories." *(He exits as "Auld Lang Syne" begins to play on the store radio.)*

    End of scene.

SCENE 3

"IN HERE IT'S ALWAYS CHRISTMAS"

A spring day in May thirty years earlier. 1992. Rachel Kaplan bounces around the store, dusting and inspecting the displays to ensure the Yuletide Cheer standard for perfection. She is the symbol of holiday cheer wearing a bold Christmas sweater with a holly brooch.

Catherine McGee enters, carrying a giant map, like one you'd get at AAA and keep in your glove compartment pre-GPS.

CATHERINE. Excuse me, I'm trying to find the Seaview Square Mall. The man at the Shell station told me to take the third left and then a right at the light but there was no light ... *(Noticing Rachel.)* And I've somehow I ended up in the North Pole.

RACHEL. *(Genuinely enthusiastic.)* Welcome to the Yuletide Cheer Holiday Store. Ho-Ho-How can I help you?

CATHERINE. You do know it's May, don't you?

RACHEL. In here it's always Christmas.

CATHERINE. I see that. So yeah - I'm trying to get to the Seaview Square Mall.

RACHEL. Oh. It's easy. You know where the Perkins is? Just go past the Perkins. Hang a left on Sycamore. Take that til you hit the circle. It's either the third or fourth turnoff - by the Exxon station - it used to be an Exxon, now I think it's a Speedway. Either way. The gas station. Take that for about a half a mile or so and then the mall will be up on the right. There will be signs. It's pretty easy.

CATHERINE. There is no way I'm going to remember all that.

RACHEL. I can repeat it. Not a problem. So you know where the Perkins is?

CATHERINE. I don't.

RACHEL. Then do you know where the K-Mart is? The Perkins is right near the K-Mart?

CATHERINE. I'm new to the area and still figuring out where everything is. Would you mind writing it down?

RACHEL. Sure thing! Let me go grab a pen and paper. *(She heads over to the register, takes out a pen and paper, and starts writing.)*

CATHERINE. Thank you. *(Looking around the store.)* So you only sell Christmas stuff here?

RACHEL. Yep.

CATHERINE. And people really buy Christmas stuff all year round?

RACHEL. They do! We actually had a women come in today who bought a dozen rolls of wrapping paper, a couple cookie cutters, and a stuffed donkey wearing a Santa hat.

CATHERINE. That's a lot of stuff.

RACHEL. I know. It surprises me too. There are some people, I think Christmas shopping stresses them out. The sooner they can check it off their list, the better. But most just come in and browse.

CATHERINE. I can see that. It's a really nice little shop.

RACHEL. Thank you! My business partner keeps wanting to add things and make it all cluttered. I keep on telling her that people associate the holidays with the crazy but they love them for their calm. So there will be no giant inflatable reindeer in here. Not on my watch. *(She finishes writing out the directions and hands them to Catherine.)* Here you go!

CATHERINE. Thank you so much. You are a lifesaver. Without you, I'd just be driving around and around until I disappeared like Amelia Earhart.

RACHEL. Before you go, can I ask you a quick question?

CATHERINE. Sure.

RACHEL. And I hope you won't think less of me for asking this.

CATHERINE. That really depends on what you're asking.

RACHEL. Fair. *(Composes herself.)* What's the deal with the donkey in the Santa hat?

CATHERINE. The deal?

RACHEL. What is it from? The donkey. I have never seen it before anywhere and I think it's a thing and it's been driving me crazy. And when the women bought it today, she was like "Oh my God! I can't believe you carry this!" and I had to be like "Of course we do!" but I have no idea what this is. A donkey in a Santa hat? Why is this something that would excite people?

CATHERINE. *(Laughing.)* Oh. It's from a song! "Dominick the Donkey".

RACHEL. "Dominick the Donkey"? I should write that down.

CATHERINE. Be careful. It's one of those songs that when you hear it, you can't unhear it. Ever.

RACHEL. I'm going to have to risk it. It's part of the job. A good chef should be familiar cooking with a whole bunch of different ingredients. Meats, vegetables, fish, grains. She doesn't have to like them all, but she's got to know what they are. I will listen to this Dexter the Donkey -

CATHERINE. Dominick.

RACHEL. Yes. Dominick. I will listen to it.

CATHERINE. Godspeed.

RACHEL. It can't be that bad.

CATHERINE. It's not my cup of tea. Fine to listen to once a year but not every day. You'll see.

RACHEL. I appreciate your help. I didn't grow up really celebrating Christmas -

CATHERINE. You didn't?

RACHEL. No, but I went to public school so I feel like I got the Cliff notes version. I had to learn a lot to manage this store. I would go to the library all the time to check out different books - the librarian calls me Mrs. Claus because I check out so many - but I need to know what I'm selling. There are so many traditions, and songs, and movies - I think I've seen at least eight different versions of *A Christmas Carol*.

CATHERINE. I've heard they are releasing one this year with the Muppets.

RACHEL. Are you serious? The Muppets?

CATHERINE. Yeah, that's what I heard.

RACHEL. That's wild. The Muppets are going to do *A Christmas Carol*. Who's next? Pee Wee Herman? Eventually it's going to come to a point where you will be considered odd if you haven't been in a production of *A Christmas Carol*.

CATHERINE. I was. Played Scrooge's sister when I was in 4th grade.

RACHEL. I played Bob Cratchit. We didn't have many boys in our high school's drama club. I looked pretty dapper in my top hat but my British accent sounded like Dick Van Dyke in *Mary Poppins*. *(In her best cockney British accent.)* "But Mr. Scrooge, sir. Tomorrow's Christmas, it is. The 25th of December. It only come round once a year, it does."

CATHERINE. Bravo!

RACHEL. So I have *A Christmas Carol* down pat. I'm just learning all the other stuff and there is so much stuff. Do you have another quick second? I feel like I'm taking up all your time.

CATHERINE. I don't, I'm sorry. I really need to get going. My son is actually out in the car -

RACHEL. Your son! You could have brought him in here.

CATHERINE. No, it's not that. He's asleep. Hugo is a ball of energy. Refuses to take naps, but in the car out like a light. And when my kid naps, I let him nap. But I don't know if you'd want him in here in any case. I could see him running around, knocking over the Christmas tree -

RACHEL. I'm sure he wouldn't.

CATHERINE. - and I would be so embarrassed. I hear a big crash and then see my son lying next to a fallen pine with ornaments scattered everywhere. If we were in a TV sitcom, I'd look around all weird and be like "Is this someone's kid?" and then we'd get that canned laughter.

RACHEL. Totally.

CATHERINE. But in real life, I can't joke like that so I'd just feel mortified. That kid is my everything even though he drives me nuts sometimes. I never want him ever to hear - even in jest - anything that implies I may be embarrassed by him … even if occasionally he makes me feel it.

RACHEL. I totally understand. I have two of my own.

CATHERINE. Two. Boys? Girls?

RACHEL. One of each. They're good kids but there are always those moments when they want to kill each other. One time, we went out to the diner and the waitress gave them crayons to color on the placemats…but there was only one red crayon. Practically started World War III. That was the first time I actually thought I'd be asked to leave a restaurant.

CATHERINE. Then you get it.

RACHEL. Any economist who wants to study supply and demand just needs to come over and babysit my kids for an afternoon. If there is only one of something- a toy, a treat, a crayon it instantly becomes the most desired treasure in the world.

CATHERINE. Absolutely. Well, thank you again for your help.

RACHEL. Before you go. One last thing.

CATHERINE. I really need to -

RACHEL. I know. I know. I just need an expert opinion on something. It'll only take a second. *(From behind the register, Rachel pulls out a Tupperware container.)* It's part of my Christmas research. I've been baking as many different Christmas cookies as possible. *(Holding out the container.)* Try one! What do you think? *(Catherine takes one and takes a bite.)* It's a Snickerdoodle. It's like if a sugar cookie got all dolled up for a night on the town. I love the name Snickerdoodle. Apparently they are from the German word "Schneckennudel" which is also fun to say.

CATHERINE. They are delicious.

RACHEL. Thanks! Take another. Take one for you son. If I keep eating all the cookies I make, I'll be able to play Santa at Christmas.

CATHERINE. These are really fantastic. I used to love to bake, but I can't remember the last time I had homemade cookies. Do you remember where you found the recipe?

RACHEL. Not offhand, but I have it at home. I can copy it for you and have it next time you stop by.

CATHERINE. Never mind then. You don't need to worry about it.

RACHEL. It's not a problem. I'd be happy to.

CATHERINE. I appreciate the offer, but honestly, I don't know when that'll be. You see - I don't really go shopping for me. I was only lost and stumbled in here looking for directions.

RACHEL. If you are worried you won't find the shop again, I can give you directions. You know where the Perkins is?

CATHERINE. No. It's has nothing to do with directions. It's just that it's only the two of us: me and Hugo. My husband was in the army and we had Hugo right before he was deployed. It was only supposed to be a year but then one afternoon a soldier comes to my door to tell me he not going to be coming home. Life is funny. You can have it all figured out: the life you want to build, the person you want to build it with. And then one knock on the door and you're alone, with a child too young to understand why, and a house that's suddenly gotten too big.

RACHEL. I'm so sorry.

CATHERINE. So now it's just me and him. And I know it's probably stupid, but with me being gone at work so much of the time, I just feel really selfish using our time together to drag him to a store for only my enjoyment.

RACHEL. I think he could entertain himself here. It's not a kid's store, but not everything's a choking hazard.

CATHERINE. He'd destroy everything. When he gets excited, he's like a hurricane of enthusiasm.

RACHEL. Does he like Christmas?

CATHERINE. It's got toys, and cookies, and pretty flashing lights. That's pretty much a four-year-old's Holy Trinity.

RACHEL. Then bring him by.

CATHERINE. You don't understand. I would be mortified if -

RACHEL. Can I offer you some advice? You can say no. I don't mean to be forward. I grew up in a family where people just give advice. They'd be like "Rachel, you know what's wrong with your Thanksgiving turkey?" And then I'd get an impromptu cooking lesson from a cousin who's never cooked Thanksgiving in her life. So I understand it can be annoying when people just throw stuff at you.

CATHERINE. No, it's okay. Please.

RACHEL. I find this works with my oldest. When I want her to stay out of trouble, I give her a job.

CATHERINE. A job? He's only four. I have to wait until he's at least six before I can get him a job in the mine.

RACHEL. Children want to help, so I find some way to make them think they are helping. A few weeks ago, I had just put my youngest down for a nap - he desperately needed one – you can just tell, but my daughter Maya wouldn't be quiet. She was singing Disney songs so loud that they could probably hear her in Disney World.

CATHERINE. That's funny.

RACHEL. So I gave Maya an incredibly important job. We have this apple tree in our backyard. The deer always eat the apples. I asked her to watch it for me. To keep a lookout and let me know the moment a deer appears. See if we could catch them in the act.

CATHERINE. And that kept her quiet for your son's entire naptime?

RACHEL. No. About 15 minutes, but that's all you'll need when you visit here, right? We'll figure out something for your son to do so that you can have a few moments to yourself.

CATHERINE. Maybe he can help me pick the perfect ornament for the tree?

RACHEL. I love it. I'd just keep him on that end of the store away from the glass ones. See that box over there? All the ones in there are a dollar.

CATHERINE. Smart. Well, I gotta get to the mall. Hugo's outgrown his sneakers and needs a new pair. Thank you, again, for the directions ... and the cookies.

RACHEL. My pleasure. And I'll have the recipe waiting for

you next time you pop by. Looking forward to meeting your son.

CATHERINE. Thanks. We'll see how it goes. *(She exits.)*

    End of scene.

SCENE 4

"YOU CAN'T UNFIGURE OUT A SECRET.
ALL YOU CAN DO IS PRETEND YOU HAVEN'T."

One year after Scene 1, a lovely spring day in May. Yuletide Cheer is now a Starbucks. Maya sits at a table, with two coffee cups in front of her. Hugo enters. The spring in his step is gone. Maya spots him right away.

MAYA. Hey, Hugo! It's me, Maya. I don't know if you remember -

HUGO. What are you doing here?

MAYA. So you do remember me.

HUGO. What are you doing here?

MAYA. Just drinking some overpriced coffee. I got one for you...in case you stopped by today. *(She hands him a cup. He suspiciously looks at it, and then as he sips it)* It may be a little cold. *(It is.)* I've been here a while. I honestly wasn't sure if you'd come.

HUGO. It's my mom's birthday. And this was the site of her favorite store. *(Sarcastically.)* I love what you've done with the place.

MAYA. Don't knock it until you've tried out the bathrooms. These have working hot water.

HUGO. Can you not with the snide comments today?

MAYA. I'm sorry. It's a thing. I try to use humor to hide

my inner guilt.

HUGO. You should feel guilty. You turned your mom's store into a Starbucks.

MAYA. We both know I didn't, but that doesn't stop me from feeling guilty. No matter what I did, I was going to let someone down. Jews don't really believe in Hell but if there was a Jewish Hell, it'd be a room full of people perpetually disappointed by every decision I make for all eternity. That's how the guilt works.

HUGO. How do you function?

MAYA. You just constantly try to find ways to relieve it. *(Maya does an over-the-top comically-fake obviously-a-signal yawn.)*

HUGO. What are you doing?

MAYA. Trying to be discreet.

HUGO. What?

MAYA. You'll see. *(Soft instrumental Christmas music starts playing in the store.)*

HUGO. Are they playing Christmas music?

MAYA. Yeah.

HUGO. It's May.

MAYA. Not in here. Here it's always Christmas.

HUGO. Sounds familiar.

MAYA. *(Confessing.)* I actually paid them.

HUGO. You paid them?

MAYA. Yeah, five-hundred dollars.

HUGO. *(Shocked.)* Are you serious? That's how you spent the money!

MAYA. No. I just asked them. Told them I had a friend stopping by who could use a little jolly. I just thought saying five hundred dollars added some nice symmetry to everything. I actually used the money on airline tickets to see my mom. Flew down to my brother's house. Saw my nieces and nephew. Had a long talk with my mom. It was nice and healthy and way overdue. It felt like, since the store was no longer anyone's burden or responsibility, we could just talk.

HUGO. Did you really wait here all day just to tell me about your mother ... on my dead mother's birthday?

MAYA. No. I didn't - I'm here because I thought you may need a little Christmas ... like the song says.

HUGO. I'm fine. The coffee's enough.

MAYA. When I was packing away the store –

HUGO. I don't want to hear about the store either.

MAYA. It's only one thing -

HUGO. No thank you.

MAYA. Just one. It's quick.

HUGO. One. That's it.

MAYA. When I was packing up the store, I came across this box. It was full of letters that kids wrote to Santa. Back from when we kept the mailbox out. Most were pretty boring - a lot of requests for Pogs - but I came across this one. *(She goes to hand Hugo the letter. He doesn't take it.)* That's fine. I can read it. *(Reading.)* "Dear Santa, I know you didn't come to my house last year. My mom tried to make me think you did, but I spotted her wrapping paper. It's okay. I'm not mad. You come to our house every year and I know I did not do enough to make it special. I'll pick a nicer ornament this year. Promise. Sincerely, Hugo." *(Maya puts the letter on the table.)*

HUGO. *(Glancing over the letter.)* My cursive was pretty good then. Probably the last time I used it.

MAYA. When I saw the letter, my first thought was "Aww. It's little Hugo! He has a surprisingly good sense of sentence structure for a 3rd grader." Then I was like "Wow, this is really sad." But then I went "Wait a minute!"

Something didn't make sense.

HUGO. Is there a point to this?

MAYA. When you came into the store - the first time- you were sitting on the floor, right over there, playing with ornaments –

HUGO. I remember.

MAYA. And you told me that you noticing your mom's wrapping paper was the glass shattering moment when you realized that Santa wasn't real.

HUGO. And?

MAYA. But you still wrote this letter.

HUGO. *(Thinks about it.)* I guess I didn't want it to be over. That's what the letter was. A last attempt. But it didn't end up mattering. You can't un-figure out a secret. All you can do is pretend you haven't.

MAYA. There's one thing I never understood about the whole Santa thing.

HUGO. What's that?

MAYA. Why?

HUGO. *(Confused.)* Why?

MAYA. Yeah. Why. Why do parents allow it to happen? Having their kids believe that their gifts are coming from some magical creature.

HUGO. It's like the Tooth Fairy.

MAYA. No. I get the Tooth Fairy. If I was buying children's baby teeth, I'd want to do that anonymously. That one's just weird.

HUGO. So you didn't believe in the Tooth Fairy either?

MAYA. No, I did. For a little bit. But then you catch onto the absurdity, yet you realize that if you say anything, it probably means the money is going to stop showing up under the pillow. I think that's when humans are taught willful ignorance. Some creature is literally harvesting children's teeth and we learn to take the money and not ask questions. But what's the purpose of Santa Claus? Rewarding obedience? Teaching kids to blindly follow Jolly Old Big Brother of the North Pole and he will bestow upon you gifts. However, if you step out of line, he'll know, and you will get coal, dinosaur remains, probably as a reminder of what happened to the last species that questioned his authority.

HUGO. That's not even close. Santa is about believing that someone out there in the world cares. Imagine opening a present, and it's exactly what you wanted, and someone knew that, and they gave it to you.

MAYA. That was my parents.

HUGO. Mine too. That someone out there in the world who cares ... often it's your parents. So yeah, after I found out that Santa was actually my mom, I was sad ... and then a little angry I went through a phase where I hardcore rooted for the Grinch to steal Christmas – but then I realized of course Santa had to be my mom. Who else would listen to me talk for hours about the board game Crossfire? The commercials made it look like it was some epic battle for the galaxy when in actuality it's just a game where you shoot marbles at a couple pieces of plastic. I would make up new lyrics to the theme song and sing them for my mom ... and she would listen. I'd remember her looking at me so attentively, like my account of this fictional board game war would go down in history like the Iliad & the Odyssey. If I went to the mall to tell Santa about Crossfire, I'd get thirty seconds tops. Santa may be patient, but he's not mom patient.

MAYA. You were lucky to have each other.

HUGO. We both were.

MAYA. Showing love under the cover of Christmas. Deep down, I think that's why my mom always needed me to work at the store. It was her way of keeping me safe. I couldn't be running from rhinos if I was working the register.

HUGO. But now that the store is closed ...

MAYA. Baby steps. Baby steps. I'm actually working at the aquarium. In the gift shop, as a compromise. It's actually at the opposite end for the aquarium from the stingrays which made my mom very relieved. I get to watch the animals during my lunch breaks and I even made friends with the guy who feeds the penguins so every now and then he lets me do it. It's not perfect, but I made a deal with my mom. I'm going to work there until I save up enough money to move to Iceland. They have a beluga whale sanctuary there.

HUGO. You won't feel guilty moving so far away?

MAYA. Okay, so I sort of lied before. I didn't use the money on airline tickets to see my mom. It was much worse than that. I bought her a new iPhone. I installed a bunch of apps on it so she can reach me in like sixteen different ways. Phone call, video call, text message, direct message, emoji – there is no hiding. I even set it so she can see when I've seen her messages, which is dangerous, but now I can be in Iceland swimming with belugas and my mom can know I'm only a click away ... and my exact coordinates within 15 feet.

HUGO. Congrats on finding Door Number Three.

MAYA. Thanks. How have you been doing ... this year? Has it gotten any easier?

HUGO. Some days I think of her more and some days I don't think about her and then feel bad for not thinking about her. But I'm adjusting ... and growing ... and trying to move forward. Looking back, it's probably a good thing you didn't take my offer to save the store.

MAYA. What caused this epiphany?

HUGO. For starters, that Star Wars figure - I don't think it's ever going to be worth twenty thousand dollars. The guy at the comic book store lied to me. It's not even remotely limited edition.

MAYA. I may be able to help with that. These aren't twenty-thousand dollars, but I did dig up something that may have some worth. *(From under the table, Maya slides the box of dollar ornaments and hands them to Hugo. He looks in the box and examines an ornament with a similar childlike wonder as he had in the opening scene. He smiles.)*

HUGO. Thank you. They're worth the world.

MAYA. I wanted to make sure you had a way to make your Christmas special.

HUGO. *(His smile suddenly starts to fade.)* This Christmas, I tried like fifteen times to replicate my mom's Snickerdoodle recipe. I couldn't do it. No matter what I did, it didn't taste like hers. Like there was something missing. And I worry while now I can taste the difference, one day I won't be able to. I'll have forgotten.

MAYA. If you need a recipe, my mom has a pretty good one.

HUGO. I'm just worried that I'm going to remember less and less as things change and I get older. She's gone, but I don't want her to disappear.

MAYA. You ever been to a Jewish cemetery?

HUGO. No.

MAYA. It's similar to a Christian one - less crosses obviously - but if you look around at the gravestones, there are no flowers.

HUGO. No flowers? That seems depressing.

MAYA. It's a cemetery. You see - flowers represent life. They are beautifully temporary. Around for a moment and then gone. So instead, when we visit a grave, we leave a stone. Just a small one. Nothing special. Whatever is lying around. We put it right on the tombstone. Stones are like memories. They're forever. What you and your mom had is not something that's going to disappear because there's a different business in these four walls or because you didn't write down her secret Snickerdoodle recipe. You created all these amazing forever memories with your mom growing up. I'm jealous. I wish I did.

HUGO. I'm sure you did.

MAYA. I don't. I thought long and hard about it. I don't have any cool memories - just boring ones. Like when I was six years old, my parents took me and my brother to Disney World. We rode on all the rides I was big enough to ride and met so many characters - my parents even took us to a special character breakfast where we could eat pancakes with Mickey and Goofy and all the princesses. Do you know the only thing I remember? The only memory that is actually mine - not one that I think I remember because I've been told the story so many times - but an actual memory. It's me, my brother, my mom and dad, sitting on a bench near the giant golf ball looking thingy in Epcot, eating Mickey Mouse ice cream pops. Seth dribbled some on his shorts and there was this bird that was staring at us hoping we'd drop it, but like Hell was I going to lose my Mickey Mouse ice cream pop. All that money spent on vacation and the one memory I have is of a five-dollar ice cream.

HUGO. I don't think your parents would want it any other way. The best memories are the boring ones. Looking back, it's what I love most about Christmas. Christmas memories are rarely cool. Cool is for the movies. Like in *Jingle All the Way*, a kid wanting a Turbo Man action figure and then learning his dad is Turbo Man, sort of. But real-life memories are boring - sitting around a dinner table, opening presents by the tree, baking Christmas cookies, building a Gingerbread house and thinking "this is the year I'll make it look too good to eat." Boring is comfortable. I think we try so hard to make a moment that we forget that we're in it. *(The two sit for a moment in silence, sipping their coffee as music plays.)*

MAYA. Do you want to grab food? I'm starving. I've been here for hours but I refuse to eat that panini that they leave sitting out the whole time.

HUGO. Sure.

MAYA. There's this Chinese place about five minutes from here. I can show you how my family used to celebrate Christmas.

HUGO. Sounds good to me.

MAYA. Then let's go. *(A jazzy "Oh Christmas Tree" plays in the Starbucks. Maya grabs the two cups and goes to throw them out. Hugo picks up the box and heads to the exit. The music changes. It's no longer Christmas music. Noticing the change, Hugo stops. He walks back to the empty table, pulls an ornament out of the box, and sets it down on the table.)*

HUGO. Happy Birthday, Mom. *(He looks up from the table, sees Maya waiting by the door. They exit.)*

END OF PLAY

NOTES

(Use this space to make notes for your production)

NOTES

(Use this space to make notes for your production)

54

ALL BARK, NO BITE
by Kara Emily Krantz
2M, 3W, COMEDY

Charlotte and Eugene live a quiet, no-nonsense lifestyle surrounded by sudoku and argyle. Robert and Bella are boisterous and messy and ridiculously in love. Then there's the neighbor, Suzanne, who basically doesn't know what's going on, but definitely has something to say about it. Sure, relationships can be exciting! They can also be confusing, unexpected, and expose us to profound emotional risk. However, relationships are almost always worth exploring, and if we're willing to be vulnerable, can fill up the empty or wounded spaces in our hearts. And if that doesn't work? Well, get a dog.

KINGDUMB
by Jonathan Cook
10M, 6W, COMEDY

There's a new King in the land that has initiated a mysterious new tax on the citizens. Outraged, the region's finest Clock fixer, aka "Time Repair Specialist", recruits some of the most unlikely rebels to help him develop a plan to overthrow the King. Their plotting takes them on a comedic journey through perilous mountain tops all the way to the palace itself where they confront this vile King face to face. Kingdumb is a medieval fantasy comedy full of absurdist humor and illogical behavior.

www.ingramcontent.com/pod-product-compliance
Lightning Source LLC
Chambersburg PA
CBHW071358200726
48294CB00004B/1212